Endorsements

Bumbles…finds her way home! is a delightful book that is perfect for a parent and child to read together! The illustrations are charming and, as the story unfolds, there are many 'teaching opportunities' that include learning geography, introducing new vocabulary, making predictions and promoting memory skills. The sweet telling of the bee's journey home encourages discussion of Bumble's fears and joys, of the importance of being kind, of taking care of one another and of growing from one's new experiences. Parents and children alike will take pleasure in sharing such a positive and uplifting story.

~Jill Stamm, Ph.D.

Faculty, Arizona State University, and Author of Bright from the Start: The Simple, Science-Backed Way to Nurture Your Child's Developing Mind from Birth to Age 3.

This is a fantastic book! Whether you're a parent reading to young kids, a child learning to read, or a teacher looking for inspirational material, *Bumbles…finds her way home!* will serve you well. I also love that by purchasing this book, you made a difference in a developing country. This is a perfect example of sustainable and leveraged philanthropy. Bumbles is not just a children's story, it's an example of global action. My kids love it and we look forward to the next book in the Bumbles series!

~Peter H. Diamandis, MD

Chairman/CEO, XPRIZE Foundation, Co-founder/Exec-Chairman of Singularity University, and the co-author of New York Times bestseller Abundance: The Future is Better Than You Think.

The Buzzzzz

Keira read your book again last night and said, "This book is so good! When is the next one going to come out?" Seriously she must have read it 10 times.
~Suzann Francone, Educator (K-8), mother and aunt

Bumbles...finds her way home! goes right into the hearts of readers. The amazing adventure starts when Bumbles finds herself far from her tiny African village. She is lost but never gives up. Life for Bumbles is all about being happy and trusting in family and friends to find her way home.
~Andrea Buonassisi, Extraordinary mother, aunt and philanthropist

This book is great for bedtime reading. My boys really like hearing about Bumbles adventures to places near and far. My youngest became more curious about the world, while my oldest was happy to try and read along. Well written and illustrated, it earns its place in the rotation of books on my children's shelf.
~Andy James, Devoted father of two

Tripp loves Bumbles. He especially likes the storm and Bumbles in the dark pics. Great job with the book! He had me read it to him 3 times today and made his momma take it home with him.
~Tina McDougall, Auntie, grandmother and kid's book author

I love the book. My son Cayden read it 3 times. He's 13. It's not just for little kids, which is so awesome. I think what you are doing is truly amazing.
~Kristen Salcito Sandquist, Mother and Co-Founder, K2 Adventures Foundation

Thank you Lori and Frances, for my signed book! It's a hit. Fabulous read.
~Sabrina Desjardins, Mommy to Princess Lillie

This is a great story with beautiful illustrations. My children are inspired by the places Bumbles gets to travel. This has become our 'go-to' book for bedtime reading.
~Cathy Matysiak, Avid reader and mother of two

The kids were reading Bumbles as we drove home from a party. We got home, but they stayed in the car in the dark garage because they just HAD to see what happed to Bumbles. Now that's a successful kid's story!
~Chris Haver, Uncle, adventurer and kid at heart

Bumbles

...finds her way home!

By Lori Losch & Frances Tieulie

Illustrations by Pascale Lafond

Dedication

We dedicate this book to those living in developing countries around the world and to the amazing people and organizations working to enhance their quality of life. Bumbles is also for everyone who wishes to be involved in a global movement of instilling hope and empowerment.

Acknowledgement

Thank you Joey Robert Parks for taking our story and adding a little buzzzzzz. We love your editing skills! Thank you Pascale Lafond for bringing our vision for each illustration to life. Thank you TRACares Foundation and Share Humanitarian Fund for partnering with us to make this book a reality.
Most of all, thank you Ken and Bradley for your unending support.
We love you.

In a small village in Africa, there lived a young honeybee named Bumbles.

1

The village was called Kafakumba (Ka-fah-koom-bah):
You spell it like this: K-A-F-A-K-U-M-B-A.

One bright, sunny morning, Bumbles woke up feeling
super hungry. I'm starving! thought Bumbles.
So she buzzed off to find a yummy breakfast.

As Bumbles zipped along, she greeted her buddies with a friendly buzz and a warm hello. Everyone was delighted to see Bumbles. And she was happy to see their smiling faces, too.

"Goodzzzzz morning, Mrs. Chicken!"

"Cluck cluck, Bumbles!"

"Goodzzzzz morning, Mrs. Cat!"

"Meow meow, Bumbles!"

"Goodzzzzz morning, Mr. Dog!"

"Woof woof, Bumbles!"

"Goodzzzzz morning, Miss Cow!"

"Moooooo!"

5

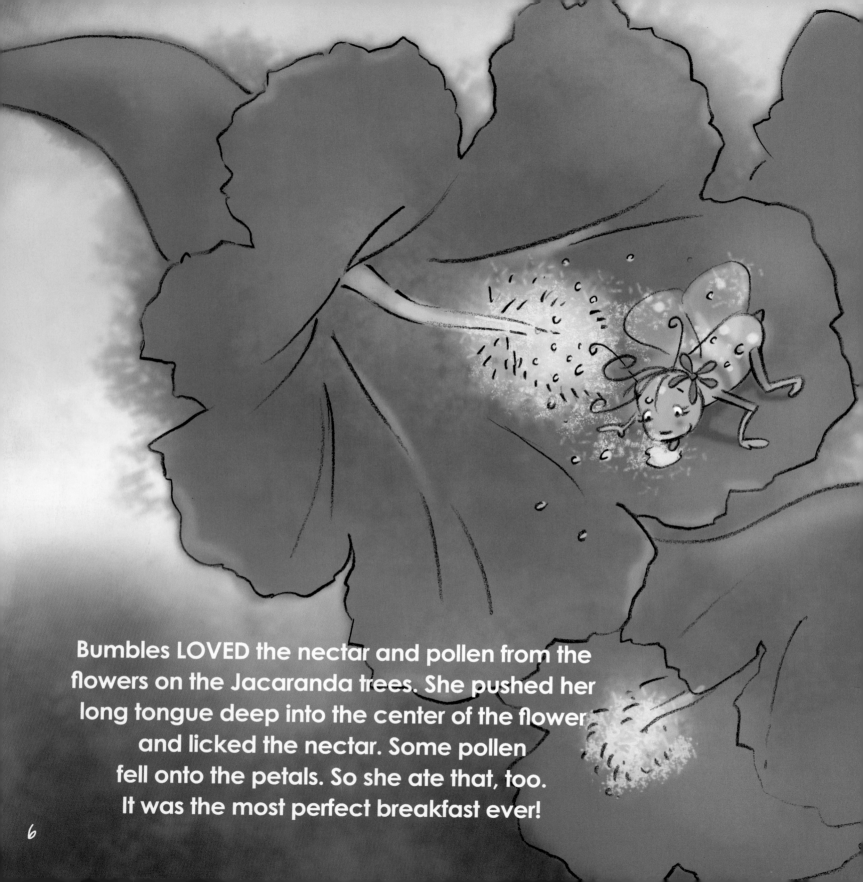

Bumbles LOVED the nectar and pollen from the flowers on the Jacaranda trees. She pushed her long tongue deep into the center of the flower and licked the nectar. Some pollen fell onto the petals. So she ate that, too. It was the most perfect breakfast ever!

6

Suddenly, heavy raindrops struck Bumbles.
"Oh, no! A storm is coming!" she cried.
Bumbles was afraid. As a baby,
she'd been stuck in a huge puddle.

Part way home, Bumbles realized she would never make it.
It was terribly rainy and windy! So she ran for cover.

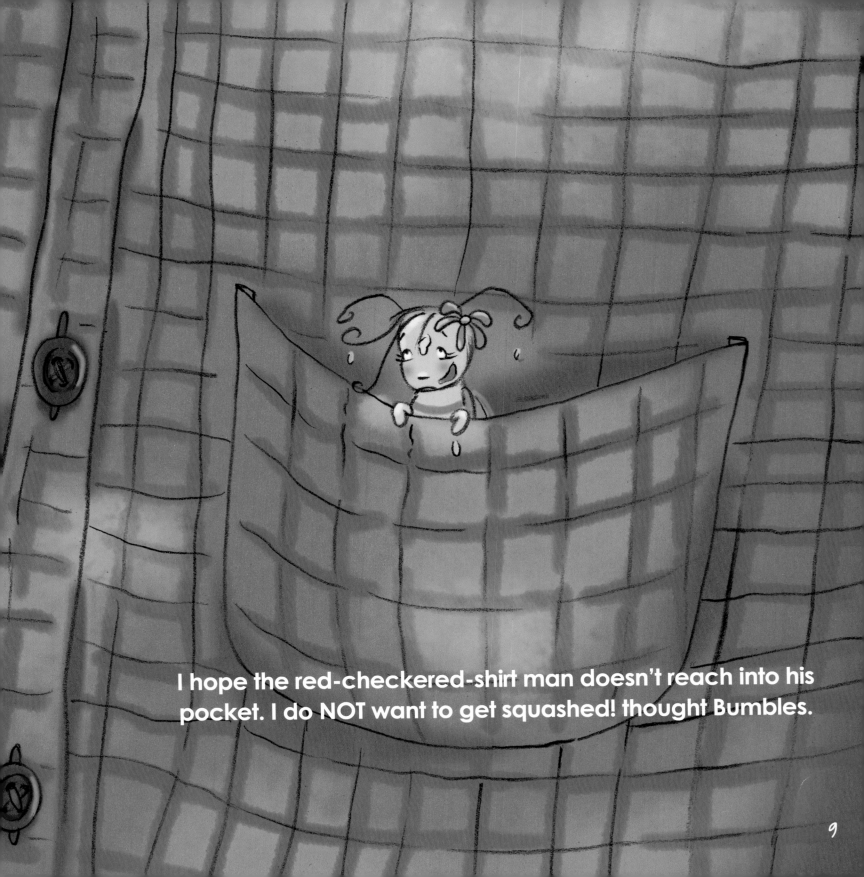

I hope the red-checkered-shirt man doesn't reach into his pocket. I do NOT want to get squashed! thought Bumbles.

"Put your ball away, kids. We have to go," said the man as he packed the last few things into a suitcase.

10

Where am I? Bumbles wondered. It's sure DARK in here!
I was in a shirt pocket ... then we went into a house ... then I
heard a clicking noise ... and now? Uh-oh. I can't move!

Bumbles heard a strange
noise getting louder and louder.
It sounded like a million, billion,
trillion honeybees.

She didn't know it, but she was flying far away from the warm African sunshine. Bumbles was heading to Whistler, Canada.

13

All Bumbles could see were huge, snow-covered
mountains. People in strange clothing were everywhere.
Nothing was familiar. Where were all her friends?
Where were the juicy Jacaranda trees?
Where was her cozy beehive?

"It's freeeeezzzzzzing!"
said Bumbles to herself.
"And I'm hungry! Hey, is that
a beehive I smell? Hooray!"

15

"Wait a minute,"
said Bumbles.
"This isn't a beehive!"

16

"Aw, come on, Dad," whined Junior goose,
as Bumbles watched curiously.
"Do we always have to pick up other
people's garbage?"

"Yes, it's good to leave a place
better than we found it,"
replied Mr. Goose.

"Oh, sheesh," said Junior,
rolling his eyes as he chucked a
coffee cup into the trashcan.

17

"Excuse me,"
said Bumbles to the Canada Goose.
"I need to go home, but I'm lost. Can you help me?"

"Why, of course little bee,"
said Mr. Goose as he lifted his wing way up into the air.
"Just crawl under here. I'll carry you home.
But you have to promise not to sting me."

"I won't sting you, Mr. Goose."

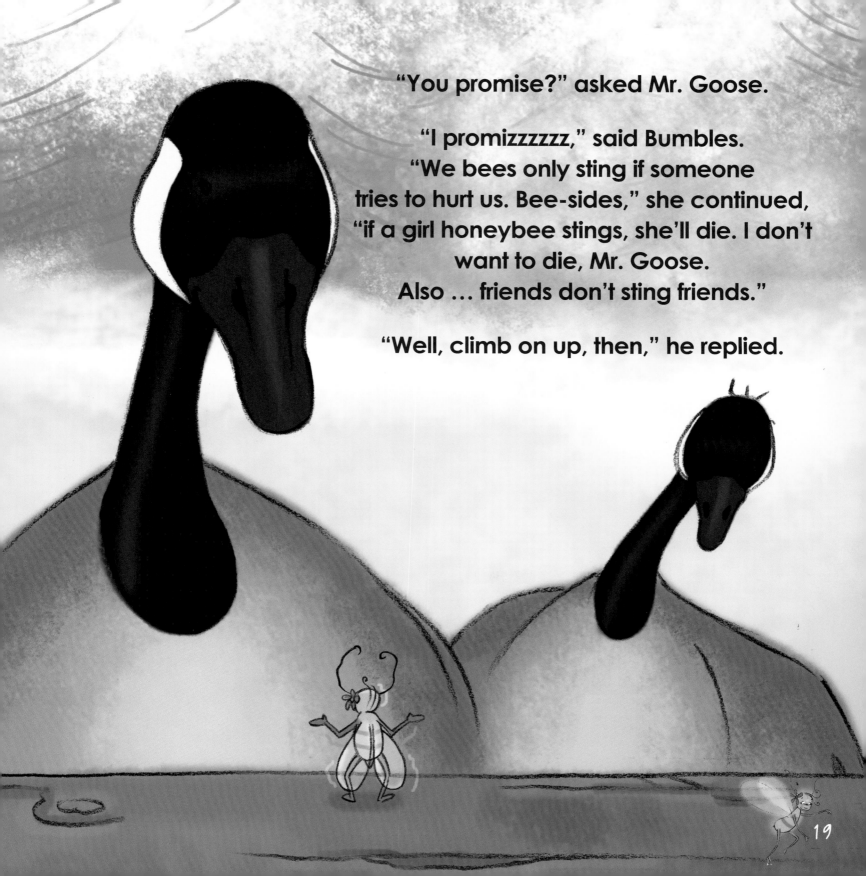

"You promise?" asked Mr. Goose.

"I promizzzzzz," said Bumbles.
"We bees only sting if someone
tries to hurt us. Bee-sides," she continued,
"if a girl honeybee stings, she'll die. I don't
want to die, Mr. Goose.
Also … friends don't sting friends."

"Well, climb on up, then," he replied.

"So, uh, where am I flying you,
little bee whose name I don't know?"

"My name is Bumbles," she said.
"Have you heard of Kafakumba?"

"Cat Fat Crumbles?" asked Mr. Goose, completely confused.
"Is that in Canada?"

"It's in Africa," said Bumbles.
"It's called Ka-Fah-Kuum-Bah.
It's a place with amazing animals, purple trees,
loads of honey ... and my home."

"I'm afraid we can't fly that far, sweet Bumbles,"
honked Mr. Goose. "But ... we can take you part way!"

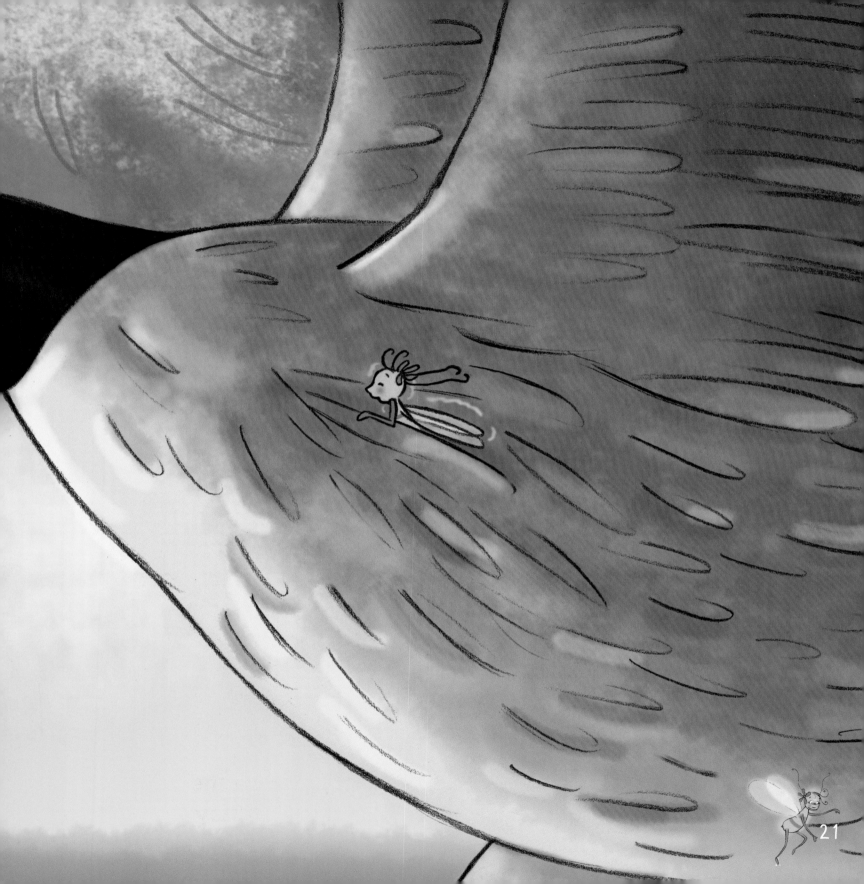

21

Mr. Goose and his family flew to sunny Florida every winter.
And, lucky for Bumbles, they were just about to take off.

So Mr. Goose teased the little bee. He playfully pinched her
with his wing-fingers and then, ZOOM! Straight up they went.

22

He was excited to help Bumbles. He could not take her all the way home, but half way to somewhere is better than all the way to nowhere.

Bumbles and her friends flew high above North America.

"What a beautiful place," said Bumbles,
peeking out from under Mr. Goose's wing.
"Before this adventure, life beyond the Jacaranda
trees was a mystery. This world is amazzzzing!"

"This is the best spot to jump off, little Bumbles,"
said Mr. Goose. "This city has lots of HUGE silver
birds that fly across the ocean.
One of those can take you the rest of the way!"

"Thanks, my friend," said Bumbles
with both sadness and glee. "You saved my life
and I'll never forget you."

"Good luck, Bumbles!" honked Mr. Goose, swelling up with
a big breath of pride. He was hopeful that his tiny travel
companion would find her way home.

Then Mr. Goose and his family swooped down into
New York City's Central Park to rest their tired wings.

Bumbles buzzed.
High in the sky, she buzzed alone.
But she was not lonely.
She was so excited about life.

27

Bumbles suddenly spotted some purple
flowers far below. Are those flowers from
a Jacaranda tree, she thought?
Her mouth started to water.
"Here I come, yummy nectar!"
cried Bumbles as she zoomed toward them.

"This is heavenly." sighed Bumbles.
"I haven't had nectar since Kafakumba!"
So she filled her hungry tummy.

29

It was her lucky day.
The hat was being sent
to its new owner in Paris.
And so was Bumbles!

JFK
AIRPORT
GATE 12

30

Then there was a loud ROAR. "Hmmm, I think I'm in one of those big birds that sounds like a zillion, trillion, mega-million beeeezzzz, again," said Bumbles.

31

Bumbles started her journey in a man's shirt pocket, lost, alone, cold and trapped. Now she was in a woman's hatbox, heading closer to home. She was warm, full and excited.

Everything was the same as before, but also
completely different. Bumbles smiled to herself,
giggling gleefully.

"Woo hoo! Fresh air at last!" said Bumbles.

34

"Excuse me, Mrs. Bird, do you know the way to Kafakumba?"

"No little bee, I've never even heard of it," she tweeted.

"Excuse me, Mr. Rabbit, do you know the way to Kafakumba?"

"Nope!" answered the jumpy jackrabbit. "But it sure sounds like a hip, hop and happy place. I hope you find it!"

"Excuse me, Mr. Butterfly, do you know the way to Kafakumba?"

m sorry," flapped the flirty butterfly. "But you're so cute. Just stay here in Paris and fly with me!"

"Um, gotta go ..."

ccuse me

Mr. Dog, do you know the way to Kafakumba?"

"Woof woof! Well, yes I do!" howled the young French Hound. "Kafakumba is where our new family lives. We can take you there!"

35

"Just hide in my ear, because most humans are afraid of you."

"I know!" cried Bumbles.
"I don't understand this. Bees are so important to humans!
Plus, we're fuzzy and cute."

"Just don't sting me by mistake," he warned.

"Not on purpose. Not by mistake. Not ever," smiled Bumbles.
"Friends don't sting friends. By the way, I'm Bumbles."

Happy to be heading home,
Bumbles settled in for the last part
of her amazing adventure.
She sighed. She smiled. She was relieved.

"We're home! We're home!"

"You're the best!" said Bumbles to Mr. Dog.
"Can I call you MD, for short?"

"Why of course, Bumbles. Can I call you B, for short?"

"Well, I'm short. And I'm a bee.
So I guess that'd beeeee okay!"

38

Bumbles was excited to share everything with her bee buddies and farm friends. So she flew off to find them.

She learned something, too. She was no longer happy just buzzing around the hive. It would always be her home, but from now on, she would fly beyond the safety and comfort of Kafakumba. She would also help others, as Mr. Goose and MD had helped her.

That thought made Bumbles go buzzzzzzzz!

The End

About Lori, Frances & Bumbles

The idea for the *Bumbles the Bee* children's book series was born after our trip to the Central African country of Zambia. We travelled to a training center located near Ndola, to bring the ladies of Kafakumba a skill that would empower them and their families with a new source of income from something they already had access to: beeswax.

We noticed several things when we'd previously visited the area: Many people in the surrounding villages live without electricity, so candles are crucial; Kafakumba has a prolific honey-making business, and literally tons of excess beeswax are produced in the process; and the Catholic Church in Africa only allows the burning of beeswax candles in its basilicas and cathedrals. Since Zambia is 25 percent Catholic, we decided to teach the villagers to use the excess beeswax to create a product they could easily sell.

So we taught them the art of candle making.

When we touched down in Zambia, we were excited to share our supplies and knowledge. We brought essential candle-making ingredients: molds of various shapes and sizes, wicks, informational packets, and seed money (which could be used to buy a stove and necessary supplies). We then held two candle-making demonstrations. The first was for leaders previously identified who would carry out the vision when we left. The second session was amazing. Three of the leaders presented the information to the broader group of villagers. We were astounded when the translator, supplied by the Ndola Business Development Center, described the detail with which Patrica, Theresa and Fosi taught the ladies in their local Bemba language. It was a beautiful time of love and empowerment, and the ladies of Kafakumba were left with a skill they could now use to earn a living.

It was a profound and blessed experience. So much so that we immediately started brainstorming ways we could showcase Kafakumba to others who might want to be involved in an important cause occurring in a remote part of the world. Our hope was that some would be able to take the Kafakumba model of empowerment and education to other countries. We thought this book would help spread that possibility.

Thank you for reading *"Bumbles … finds her way home!"* to your kids and to yourself. You're changing lives, as for every 10 copies sold, we're donating a beehive to another hardworking Zambian family.

This enriches everything.

Lori & Frances

To learn about our other philanthropic activities, to order further copies of this book, or for information on the release of Bumbles' next adventure, please visit www.Bumbles.co.

Bee-Inspired by The Lundus

Edwin Lundu was one of the fortunate kids in Zambia: he attended school. Until grade nine that is, when he had to drop out to tend the family farm. Through his teens, 20s and 30s, he eked out a living as a small-scale farmer with no real hope for a better future. In his mid-30s, he married Bridget and, in time, they had three kids. They all survived on their tiny vegetable garden. The Lundus consumed most of the food they produced and sold the excess for about $20 a month.

Poverty and hunger were their constant companions. In 2008, their luck changed. Edwin heard about Kafakumba's honey program and expressed an interest in the work. Bee Sweet took Edwin on as a pupil, and Horst, the head of the honey operation, taught him the art of beekeeping. Like all new keepers at Bee Sweet, Edwin was given five beehives to start, but he was such a gifted beekeeper that he was soon running 40 beehives of his own. As the honey program matures, that number will continue to increase!

Shortly after Edwin embarked on his new venture, he was recognized as a leader in the Luankuni area. He was selected by this local group of beekeepers to be their supervisor. Today, Edwin keeps very busy tending his farm and his beehives, and makes daily rounds to teach and help other beekeepers with their bee-keeping businesses. Mrs. Lundu helps Edwin harvest, clear and maintain their hives; works the family farm; and raises the children. They are a happy and prosperous family and strong leaders in their community.

What a marked contrast from their lives as poverty-stricken sustenance farmers! Not only do they provide for their family from the garden and the sale of excess food, they also receive about $150 a month for Edwin's managerial work. His pay is based on 10 percent of the honey produced among his beekeepers, so this amount will increase considerably as the

honey project expands. In addition to Edwin's management income, the Lundus receive money from Bee Sweet, which also purchases their honey in bulk, processes it, bottles it, and sells it wholesale to local retailers.

Last year, the Lundu's honey generated approximately $1,200 of extra personal income. The Lundus are now considered a wealthy family by Zambian standards, and an extremely wealthy family in the eyes of local villagers.

When Edwin was asked what the beekeeping business meant to him, he said, "It is perfect. It has changed everything in my life for the better." And that's what it's all about.

*To support this important effort financially, please visit www.TRACares.org. TRACares is an Arizona based 501(c)(3) whose mission is to empower community, both locally and globally. All donations are tax deductible in the US and your entire donation will be forwarded to the Enrights to be disbursed. Just $20 will provide a beehive to another Zambian family.

You can support this and other global empowerment efforts by donating through **www.Bumbles.co.**

Vision & Background of the Kafakumba Training Center

The Kafakumba Training Center was born inadvertently from the harsh realities of Central Africa…

Poverty.
Disease.
Suffering.
Hopelessness.

All are incredibly obvious throughout the region, but poorly understood and hard to rectify. Governments, non-governmental organizations, and church groups spend billions on relief, but very little ever changes. Why? Because handouts don't work. They discourage people from rising above a poverty mentality, and they don't provide any revenue-generating skills. If a society is ever going to be transformed, education and empowerment must play key roles.

With this in mind, John and Kendra Enright built the Kafakumba Training Center in 1999, just outside Ndola, Zambia. They'd had great success in various industries and ministries in the Congo going back to 1973. So when they moved to Zambia, they used their experience and knowledge to create infrastructure and activities in and around Kafakumba.

Today, the Enrights have a flourishing pastor's school and Women's Empowerment Center. They also partner with Zambians on a number of economic development projects, including: woodworking, aloe vera and banana plantations, fish farming, cattle rearing, bee keeping and chicken farming. These enterprises are powerfully changing tens of thousands of lives. A region that once boasted the worst statistics in HIV/AIDS, poverty, crime, infant mortality and other life-threatening issues is now flourishing with…

Life.
Hope.
Industry.
Abundance.

Drive through the area surrounding Kafakumba and you can sense a difference. A quick chat with the locals confirms this. So many, once downtrodden and hopeless, are actively engaged in life! One of the most significant and impactful branches of Kafakumba is its honey operation. Historically, the most popular technique for collecting the sweet nectar was "bark hiving." In this process, villagers harvest honey from a naturally formed tree hive, but usually end up destroying its host at the same time. This is an unsustainable practice that results in inconsistent harvests.

When the Enrights saw this opportunity, they acted. They secured a grant from the German government and formed Kafakumba's Bee Sweet Honey Company. Within a few years, Bee Sweet had manufactured 7,000 state-of-the-art "top bar" beehives, resulting in an annual harvest of 20 tons of honey from just 700 of those hives!

That's great news for the locals, as honey is a staple of the Zambian diet. More importantly, dozens of woodworking jobs were created. In the following

continued from page 43

few years, an additional 18,000 hives were built and inhabited and expansion still continues. This has impacted thousands of lives, as numerous bee-keeping careers have been launched as a result.

Bee Sweet does much more than create jobs. It trains each family where to place their hives to maximize honey production. It also assists them in cleaning and maintaining their hives and harvesting the honey semiannually. Bee Sweet then pays each family for their honey, processes it, and sells it through local and regional markets. Plans for sales expansion into European and North American markets are under way.

This cyclical model allows Zambian villagers to partner with Bee Sweet. Empowerment and income are the natural byproducts. Once a family has proved its reliability, Bee Sweet gives them additional hives, expanding their income even further.

Kafakumba Training Center's ultimate goal is to use empowerment to duplicate itself throughout Central Africa. When the Enrights speak of empowerment, they mean teaching, training, financial investment, successful business creation and synergistic working relationships.

We wrote *"Bumbles … finds her way home!"* to share with every reader the outstanding impact the Enrights and their supporters are having on the lives of thousands of Zambians.

We hope you've been inspired!

For more information about the Enrights and Kafakumba, please visit **www.Kafakumba.org**.